Postman Pat's Bouncy Special Delivery

Illustrations by Artful Doodlers

EGMONT

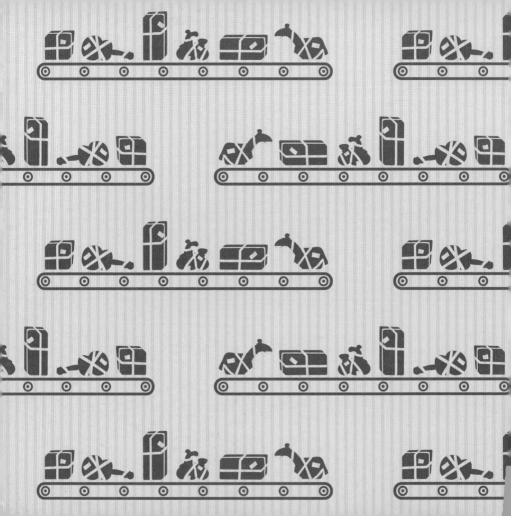

Back at the mail centre, Postman Pat, Ben and PC Selby were trying to squeeze the castle into the van.

"It's no good," puffed PC Selby. "It's never going to fit."

"I know what to do!" cried Postman Pat. "This is a job for the Special Delivery Service helicopter! Come on, Jess!"

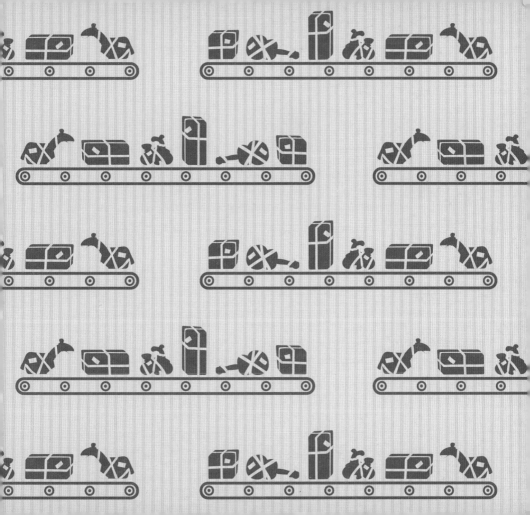

EGMONT

We bring stories to life

First published in Great Britain 2009 by Egmont UK Limited
The Yellow Building,1 Nicholas Road, London W11 4AN

Postman Pat® © 2009 Woodland Animations Ltd, a division of Classic Media Limited.
Licensed by Classic Media Distribution Limited. Original writer John Cunliffe.
Royal Mail and Post Office imagery is used by kind permission of Royal Mail Group PLC.
All rights reserved.

ISBN 978 1 4052 4579 1

46179/6

Printed in Italy

Egmont is passionate about helping to preserve the world's remaining ancient forests.
We only use paper from legal and sustainable forest sources.

This book is made from paper certified by the Forest Stewardship Council® (FSC®),
an organisation dedicated to promoting responsible management of forest resources.
For more information on the FSC, please visit www.fsc.org. To learn more about
Egmont's sustainable paper policy, please visit www.egmont.co.uk/ethical

MIX
Paper from
responsible sources
FSC® C018306

Everyone gets a fright when Postman Pat's parcel grows to an enormous size! Postman Pat will have to work hard if he wants to prove that no job is too big for the Special Delivery Service!

Postman Pat was delivering a large parcel to Michael at the mobile shop.

"Oh no! They've sent me too many!" said Michael, as boxes of plasters tumbled out all over the floor.

Just then, Pat's phone rang its special ring.

"Special Delivery Service, Postman Pat speaking," he answered.

"You need to come quickly," said Ben's voice. "I've an urgent parcel for delivery."

When Postman Pat arrived at Pencaster Mail Centre, Ben showed him the parcel for special delivery.

"There's no label on it, Pat," said Ben. "I don't know who it's for."

Suddenly, the parcel started squeaking and wriggling around. Jess jumped up in surprise.

"Look out!" shouted Postman Pat, as the parcel started to grow!

Meanwhile at the school, the children were all getting ready for their end of term party.

"Has the bouncy castle arrived yet, Mrs Taylor?" asked Julian, excitedly.

"Not yet," she replied.

Julian and Lizzie looked disappointed.

"Don't worry," said PC Selby. "I'll drop into Pencaster and check it's on its way."

At the mail centre, Ben's computer told him that the castle was for the school.

"This is certainly the biggest special delivery challenge I've ever had," said Postman Pat. "Let's get the air out to make it easier."

But they couldn't find the air valve and no matter how hard they tried to push, or squash, or even run at the castle, they just bounced off again!

When PC Selby arrived at the mail centre, he was very surprised to see the bouncy castle, on a fork-lift, being squeezed out of the loading bay.

He jumped out of the way just in time, as it popped into the yard.

"Using the fork-lift was a great idea, Pat," said Ben. "But how are we going to get it into the van?"

At the school, the party was nearly ready. Ted was clearing leaves using his powerful leaf blower.

"I do hope the bouncy castle will be here soon," said Lauren Taylor.

"I hope Pat's not getting into difficulties," worried Ted. "He's never had to deliver anything like this before."

The children couldn't believe their eyes when they saw a helicopter coming.

"What's that?" gasped Julian.

"It's our bouncy castle!" cried Lizzie.

"Special delivery, for Mrs Taylor!" Postman Pat shouted down.

"Just in time," said Lauren. "Postman Pat has saved the day!"

Postman Pat lowered the castle to the ground and landed his helicopter nearby.

But suddenly there was a loud hissing noise. Jess was bouncing up and down on the castle and his sharp claws were making holes everywhere!

"Meow," said Jess sadly, looking at the deflated castle.

"What are we going to do now?" asked Meera.

"We'll need something to cover all of these holes," said Ted.

Suddenly, Postman Pat had a good idea. He raced over to Michael's mobile shop.

"I need all of those plasters," announced Postman Pat.

"All of them?" gasped Michael in surprise.

The children helped Postman Pat stick plasters over the holes.

"Well done, Pat! It looks like it's fixed," said Lauren. "But how are we going to blow it up again?"

"I've found the air valve!" called Lizzie.

"Ah! Can we borrow your leaf blower, Ted?" asked Postman Pat.

"Pleased to help," replied Ted.

The bouncy castle was blown up again in no time. The children couldn't wait to jump on it. Even Jess was allowed to play, with Julian holding him in his arms.

"Thank you, Pat!" laughed the children, as they bounced up and down.

"No problem!" replied Postman Pat. "Special Delivery Service – mission accomplished!"

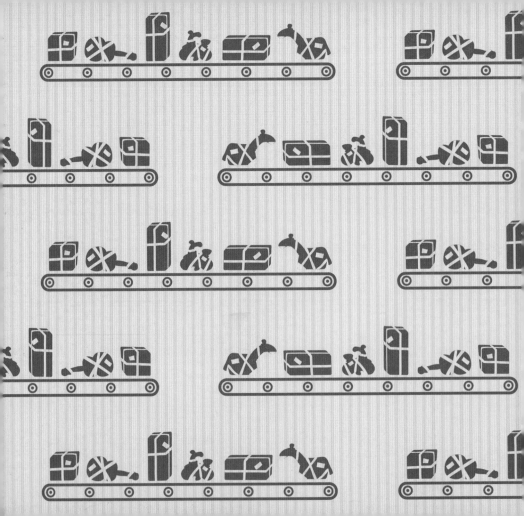